THE VERY LAST CASTLE

WORDS BY **TRAVIS JONKER**
PICTURES BY **MARK PETT**

Abrams Books for Young Readers
New York

In the middle of a small town stood something
you might not expect.

A castle.

It was, in fact, the very last castle. There had been others, but over time they had all been taken down, or fallen apart, or been destroyed. All but one. For reasons no one could remember, no one ever came out.

And no one was allowed in.

Up in
the tower,
the guard
watched the
townspeople
silently
pass by.

Then there was Ibb.

Every day she walked
past the castle, all alone.
Every day she stopped.

She looked up. She saw the
lone guard, standing stone-still.

PLUNK

Since no one had been inside the castle, the townspeople had ideas about who—or what—was in there.

SNAP

SNAP

SNAP

"Monsters," said Miss Wicks.

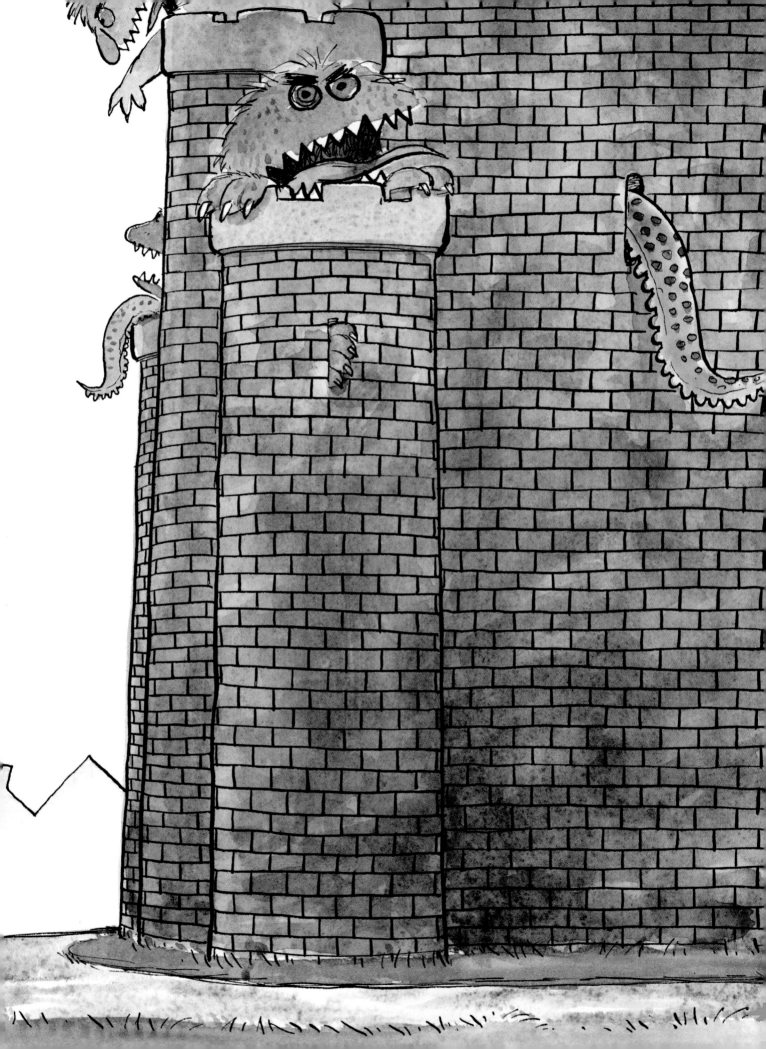

THUD
THUD
THUD

"Giants," said Alex.

H I S S
H I S S
H I S S

"Snakes," said Ibb's grandfather.

*Maybe it's something terrible, Ibb thought one day,
but maybe it's something else.*

PLUNK

The next morning, Ibb walked past the castle. She stopped and looked up at the tower.

No guard.

Ibb had an idea.

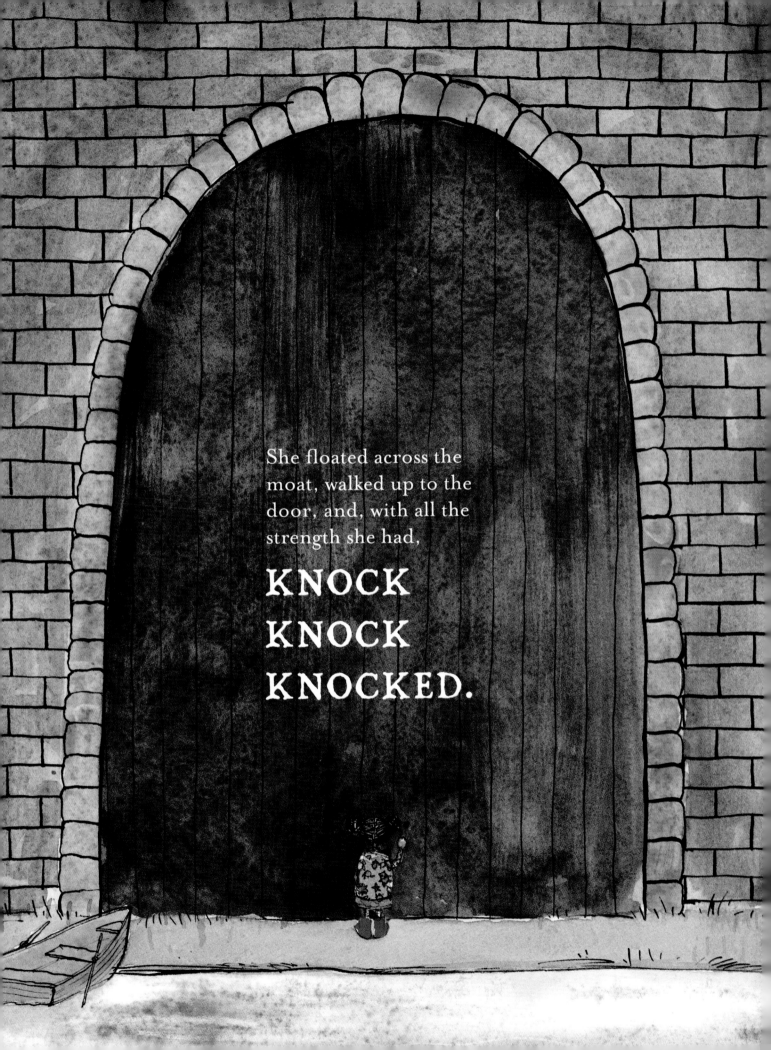

She floated across the
moat, walked up to the
door, and, with all the
strength she had,

**KNOCK
KNOCK
KNOCKED.**

Ibb didn't stop running until she was sitting in her desk at school—scared and out of breath.

Maybe Grandpa was right.

She didn't tell anyone what had happened.

Not long after, an envelope arrived.
Inside was an invitation:

Your presence is requested
at the
front gate of the castle
on
Sunday
at noon.

Everyone told Ibb to stay away.
"Monsters," said Miss Wicks.

"Snakes," said
her grandfather.

"Giants," said Alex.

Maybe it's something terrible,
Ibb thought.
Could it be something else?

On Sunday, Ibb stood
all alone outside the
front gate.

With a loud **THUNK**,
the drawbridge began to lower.
She trembled. She looked
up at the tower.

Empty.

She took a deep breath. Slowly, Ibb did something none of the townspeople had ever done—she walked inside.

It turned out Miss Wicks and Alex had been right. There *were* monsters.

And there *were* giants.
But . . . no snakes.

"Welcome," came a
voice. A kind voice.
It was the guard.

He removed his helmet. He was
much older than Ibb had expected.

"I'm the last one left.
May I show you around?"

For the rest of the day, Ibb and the guard—his name
was William—visited every corner of the castle.

Before long, they were pruning near the great hall.

SNAP

SNAP

SNAP

And harvesting by the palace.

THUD
THUD
THUD

They ended up where they had started.

"Why now?" asked Ibb.

"All the other castles are gone," answered William. "Someday I will be, too. I want someone brave to take my place. Someone curious. Will you help me?"

Ibb thought about William, all on his own.
She thought about her family and friends
outside the castle.

She thought.

And then, she knew.

"Yes," Ibb replied,
"but I have a request."

In the middle of a small town stood
the very last castle.

Sometimes, someone came out.

And everyone
was welcome in.

For Allison
– T.J.

For Cleo
– M.P.

The art in this book was completed
with pen and ink and watercolor.

Cataloging-in-Publication Data has been applied for
and may be obtained from the Library of Congress.

ISBN 978-1-4197-2574-6

Text copyright © 2018 Travis Jonker
Illustrations copyright © 2018 Mark Pett
Book design by Mercedes Padró

Printed and bound in China
10 9 8 7 6 5 4 3 2 1

Abrams Books for Young Readers are available at special discounts when
purchased in quantity for premiums and promotions as well as fundraising or
educational use. Special editions can also be created to specification.
For details, contact specialsales@abramsbooks.com or the address below.

ABRAMS The Art of Books
195 Broadway, New York, NY 10007
abramsbooks.com